This book belongs to:

....

....

For Serena, the original Little Bear and Mom,
for her love and inspiration ~ SQ

Here's to a wonderful and colorful year of spending
time in the company of good friends and family ~ CP

A NEW BURLINGTON BOOK
The Old Brewery
6 Blundell Street
London N7 9BH

Editor: Alexandra Koken
Designer: Verity Clark

First published in the United States by
QEB Publishing, Inc., 3 Wrigley, Suite A, Irvine, CA 92618

www.qed-publishing.co.uk

A CIP record for this book is available from the Library of Congress.

ISBN 978 1 78171 380 8

Printed in China

Little Bear
and the
Butterflies

Susan Quinn and Caroline Pedler

NEW
BURLINGTON
BOOKS

Little Bear was trying to
catch a butterfly.

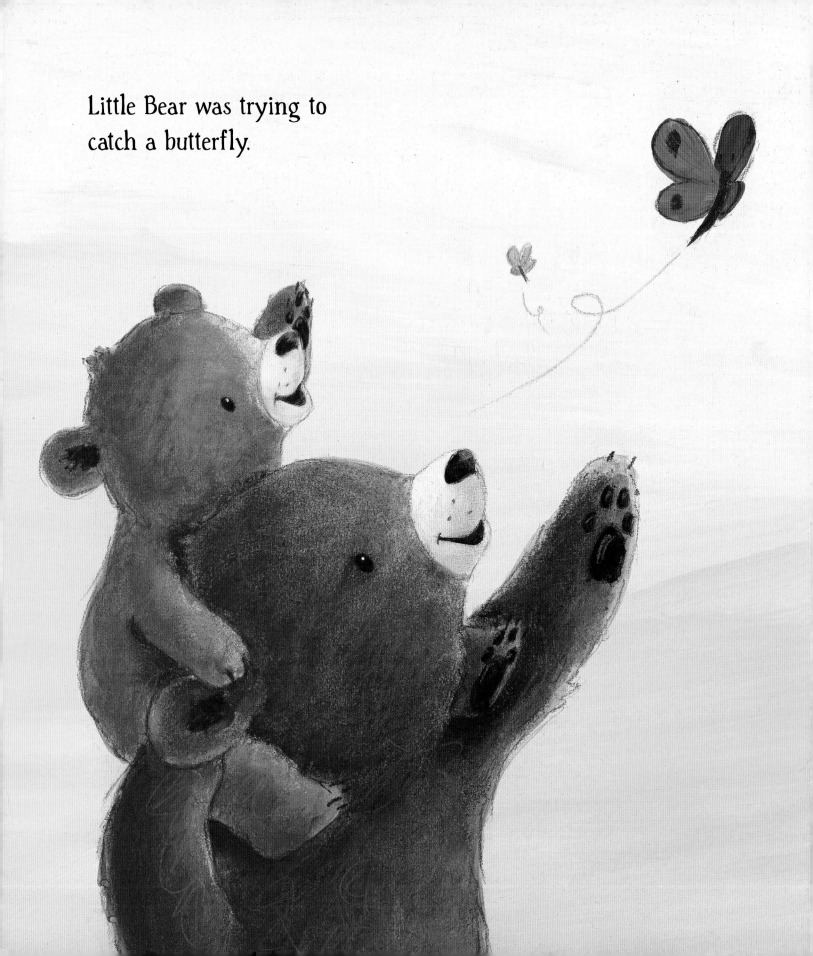

"When I was little, chasing butterflies in Bluebell Meadow was my favorite game," said Mommy Bear.

Little Bear yawned.
"Can I go to Bluebell Meadow?"

"Later," said Mommy Bear.
"But now it's time for your nap."

Little Bear was almost asleep
when something tickled her nose.

It was a butterfly!

Little Bear stood up
and stretched.

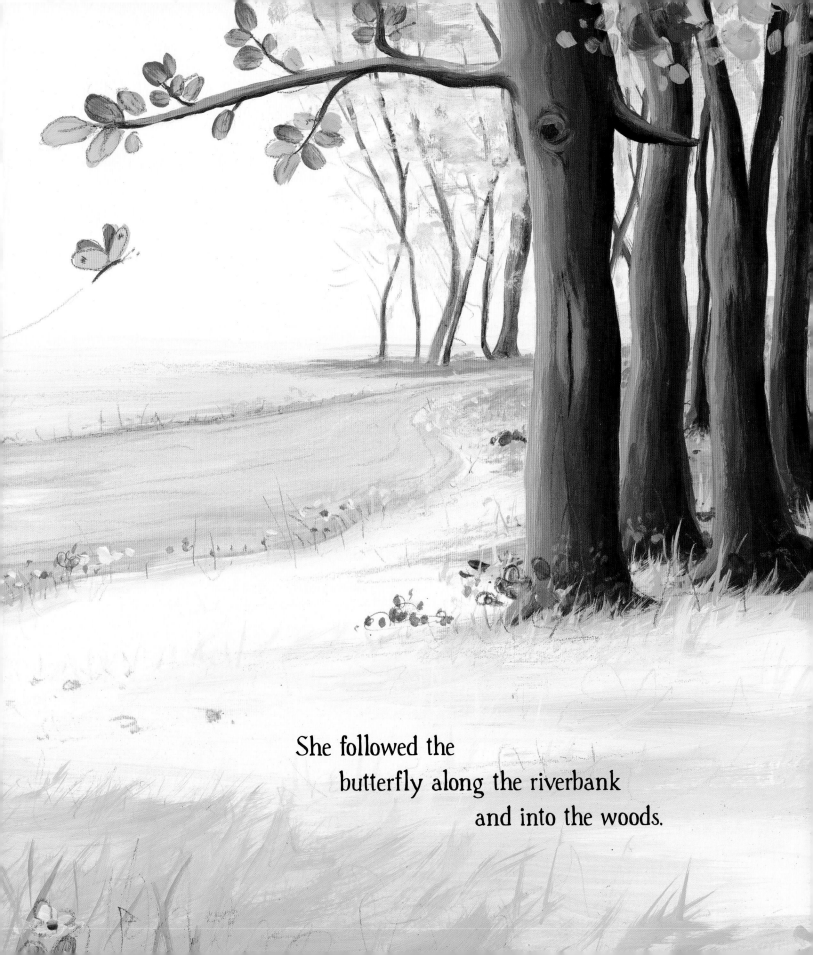

She followed the
butterfly along the riverbank
and into the woods.

Little Bear tripped over a
tree root and landed on
her bottom.

"Watch out!"
shouted Rabbit.

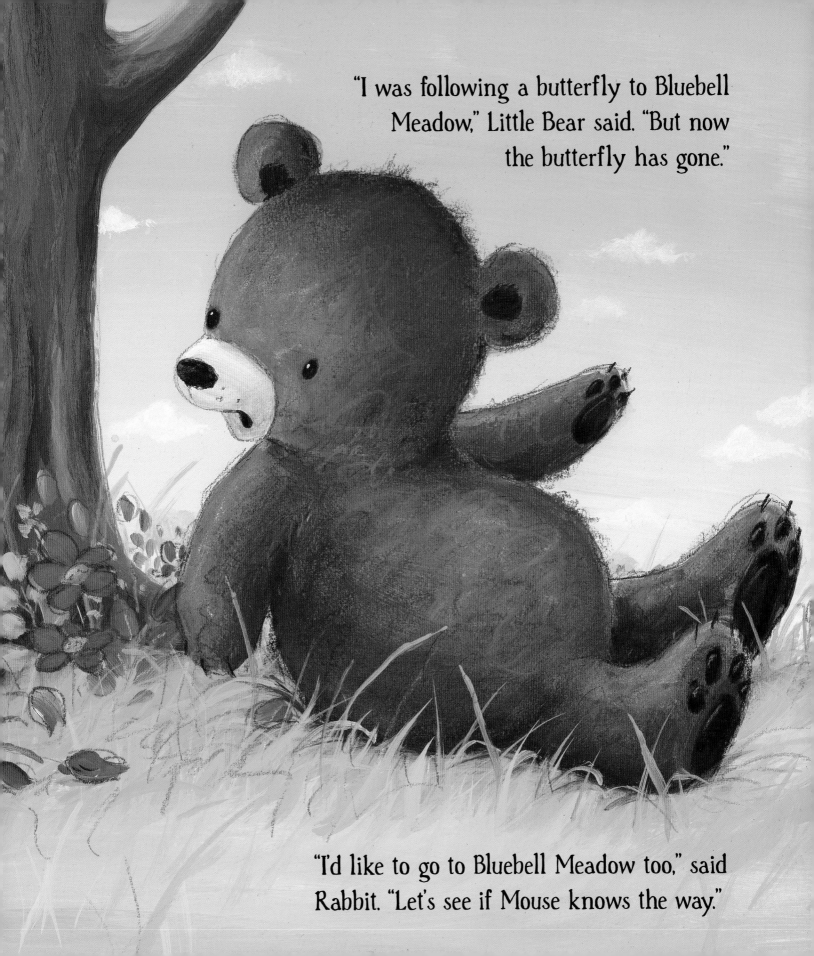

"I was following a butterfly to Bluebell Meadow," Little Bear said. "But now the butterfly has gone."

"I'd like to go to Bluebell Meadow too," said Rabbit. "Let's see if Mouse knows the way."

"Oh, hello," said Mouse.
"I'm just piling up leaves to
bounce on. Would you like
to help me?"

"We'd love to," said Little Bear.
Soon there was a mountain
of leaves higher than
Mouse and Rabbit.

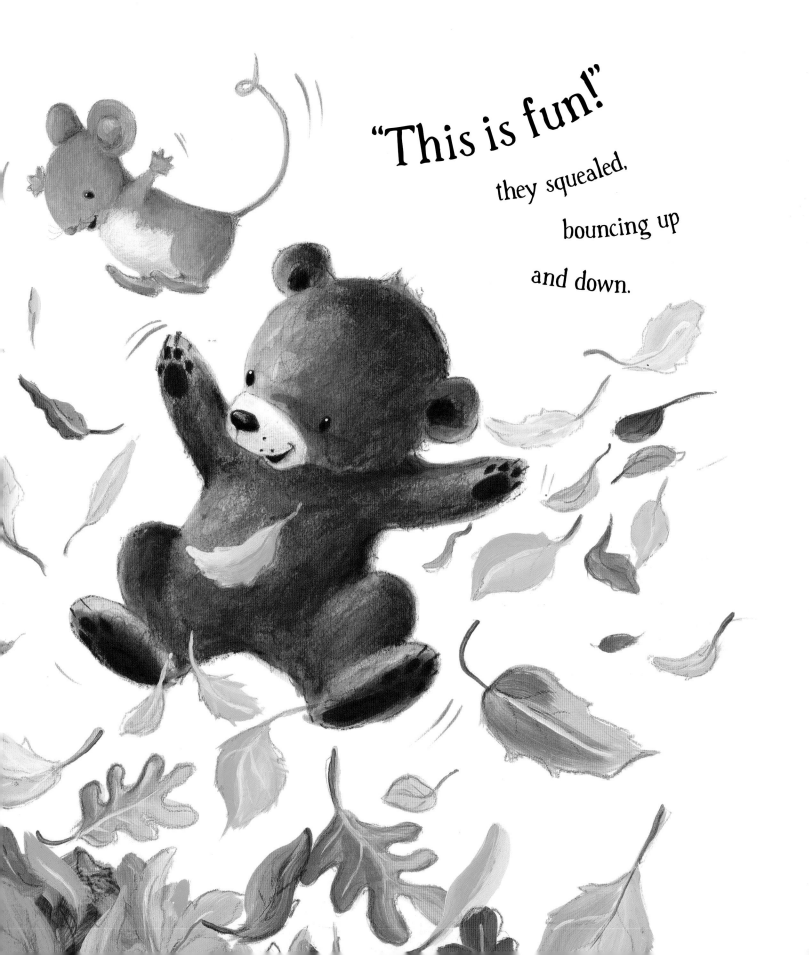

"This is fun!"
they squealed,
bouncing up
and down.

"Now we need to find Bluebell Meadow,"
Little Bear explained to Mouse.

"Let's ask Owl," said Mouse.
"He knows everything."

So Little Bear
    climbed Owl's tree. . .

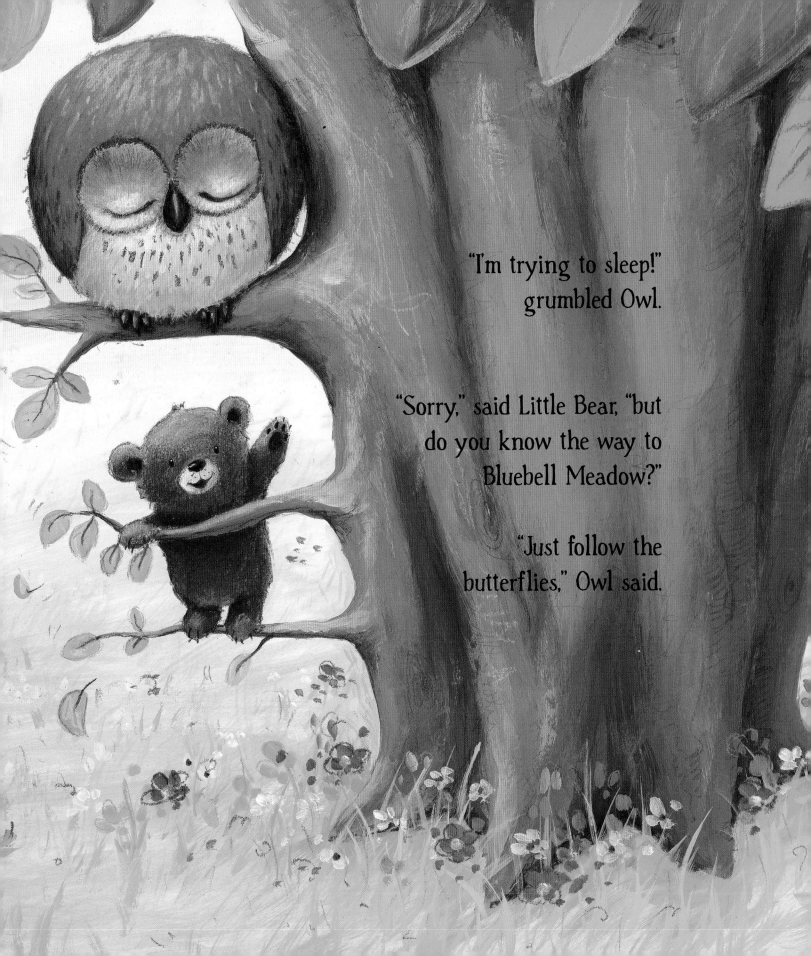

"I'm trying to sleep!"
grumbled Owl.

"Sorry," said Little Bear, "but
do you know the way to
Bluebell Meadow?"

"Just follow the
butterflies," Owl said.

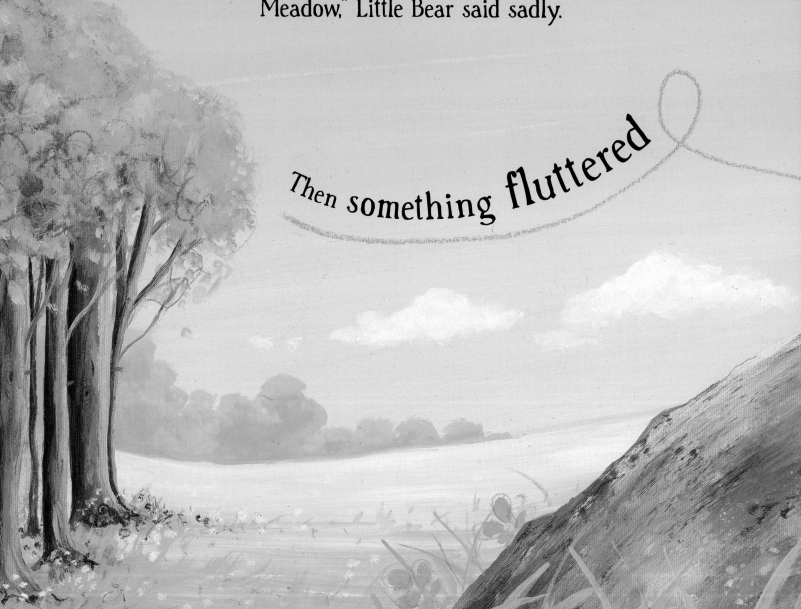

Little Bear, Rabbit, and Mouse sat on
a rock and waited for butterflies.

And waited.

"I don't think we'll ever find Bluebell
Meadow," Little Bear said sadly.

Then something fluttered

past her nose.

"A butterfly!" squeaked Mouse.
"Quick!" cried Little Bear, jumping to her feet.

Little Bear, Rabbit, and Mouse
followed the butterfly through
the woods.

They followed it up the hill,
and down the other side.

And when they got to
the top of the next hill, they saw. . .

...a meadow of bluebells and

butterflies dancing in the sunlight.

"We found Bluebell Meadow!"
shouted Little Bear.

They played **hide-and-seek**
among the bluebells.

They played **peekaboo**,
and made daisy chains.

But mostly they chased the butterflies.

"This is the best day ever!" Rabbit said flopping on the grass.

"I could stay here forever," said Little Bear sleepily.

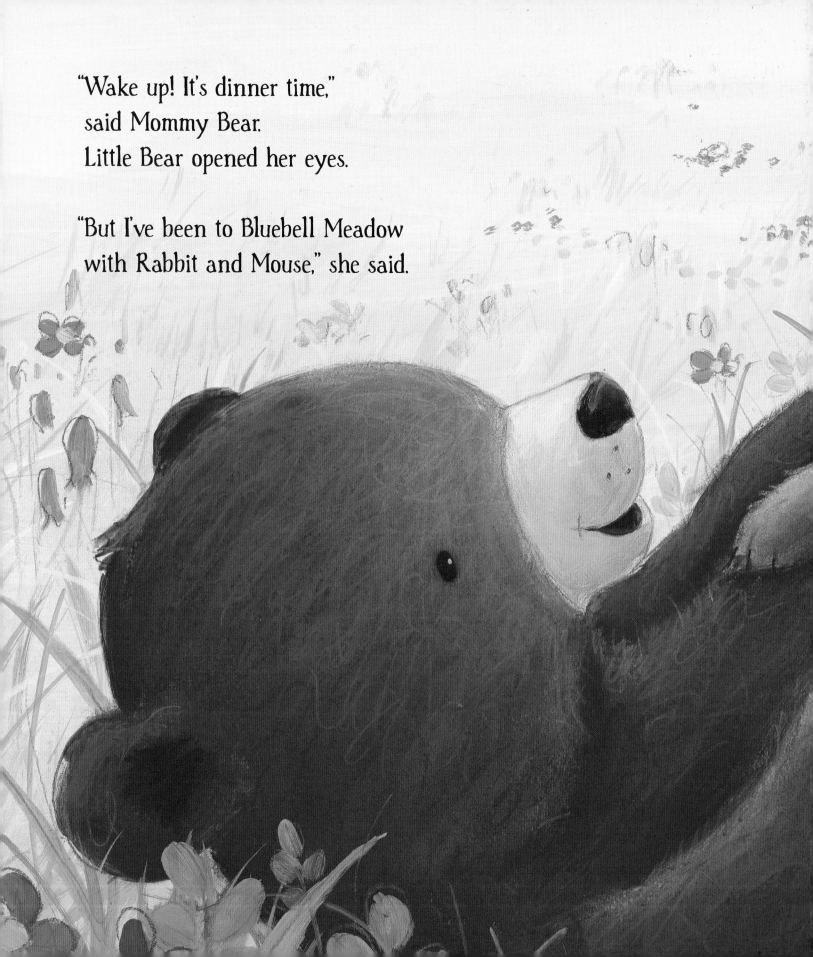

"Wake up! It's dinner time,"
said Mommy Bear.
Little Bear opened her eyes.

"But I've been to Bluebell Meadow
with Rabbit and Mouse," she said.

"It was just a dream," said Mommy Bear.
"It seemed so real!" said Little Bear.
"Good dreams are like that," Mommy Bear
said, giving her a great big bearhug.

Next steps

Show the children the cover again. What did the children think the book would be about before they heard the story? How is the story different?

Why do the children think Little Bear and Rabbit helped Mouse make his pile of leaves? Ask the children to talk about an occasion when they helped one of their friends. What did they do? How did it make them feel?

Why do the children think Owl was grumpy? Ask the children why Owl was trying to sleep in the middle of the afternoon. Ask them how they feel if they are woken up suddenly.

Ask the children to talk about their best day ever. What made it so special?

Ask the children to draw and cut out paper butterflies. Perhaps arrange them into sizes and colors and ask the children to count them.

Look at the picture of Little Bear on the last page. Ask the children whether they can see a difference between Little Bear here and in the first picture in the book. Can they suggest why she is wearing a daisy chain around her neck in the last picture?

Ask the children if they think Little Bear's trip to Bluebell Meadow was a dream or a magical adventure. If it was magic, do the children think Mommy Bear might be magical? Or the butterfly?